HOW TO ACCEPT NO

by Michael Gordon

© 2020 Michael Gordon. All rights reserved.

All rights reserved. This book or parts thereof may not be reproduced in any form, stored in any retrieval system, or transmitted in any form by any means—electronic, mechanical, photocopy, recording, or otherwise—without prior written permission of the publisher, except as provided by United States of America copyright law

THIS BOOK BELONGS TO

....

....

AGE: ....

When Mom and Josh were shopping at the grocery store, Josh got fed up — he didn't want to be there anymore.

As Mom stood in the long check-out line so she could pay,
Josh complained that shopping was ruining his day.

"I'm sorry to hear that, but we can't leave just yet."

Josh didn't like Mom's response and got quite upset.

"I want to go home now! I don't like this place!"

Josh clenched his fists into balls and got red in the face.

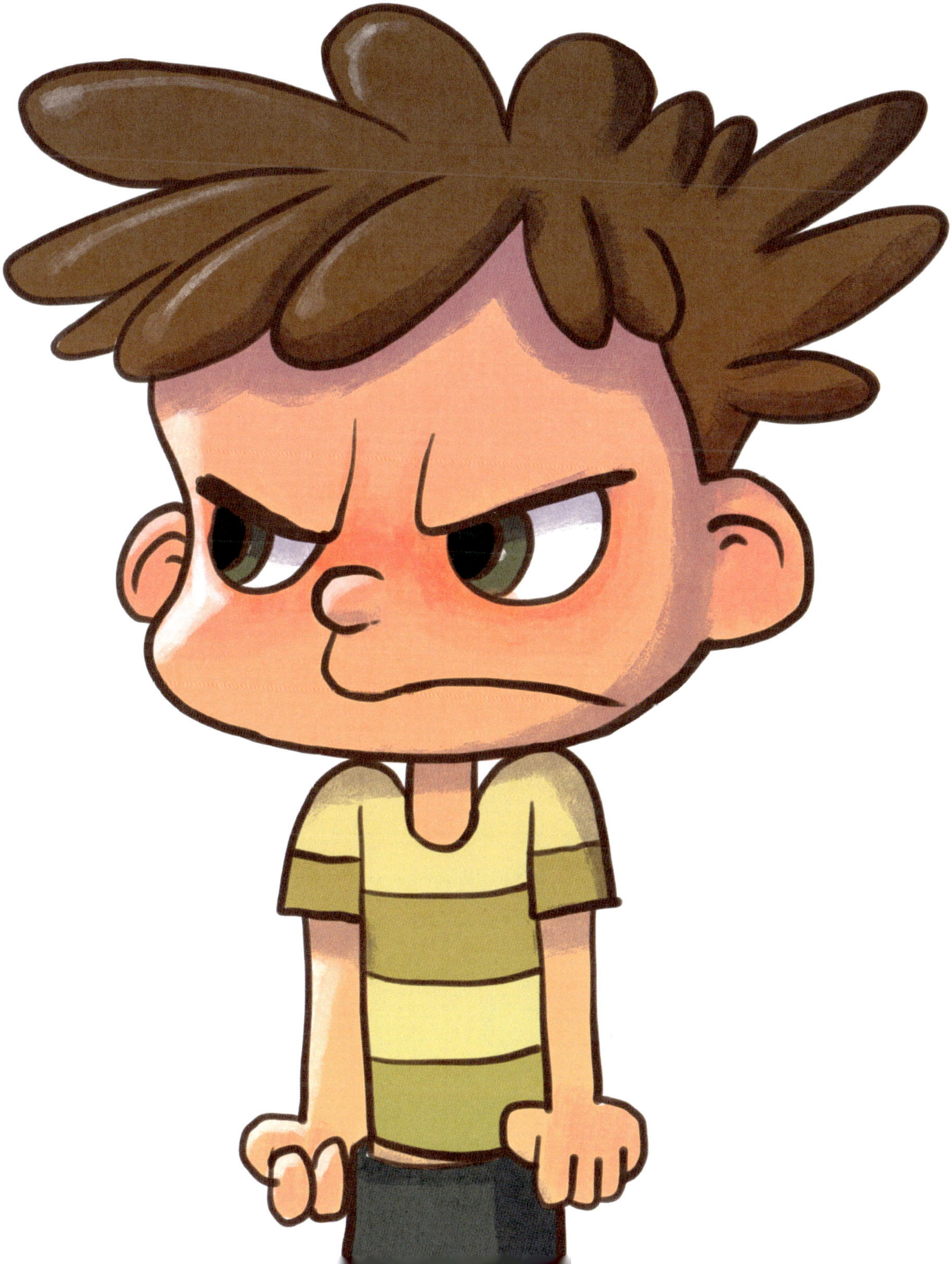

Mom kindly bent down, smiled at Josh and stroked his head.

"It's hard to wait when you don't want to," she said.

"Sometimes waiting makes me feel impatient too.

When I feel angry, Josh, do you know what I do?"

"I get rid of those feelings by stomping on the floor.

I imagine I'm a T-Rex — a big dinosaur."

So, Josh tried stomping like a big beast might do.

When he felt better, he went back to Mom in the queue.

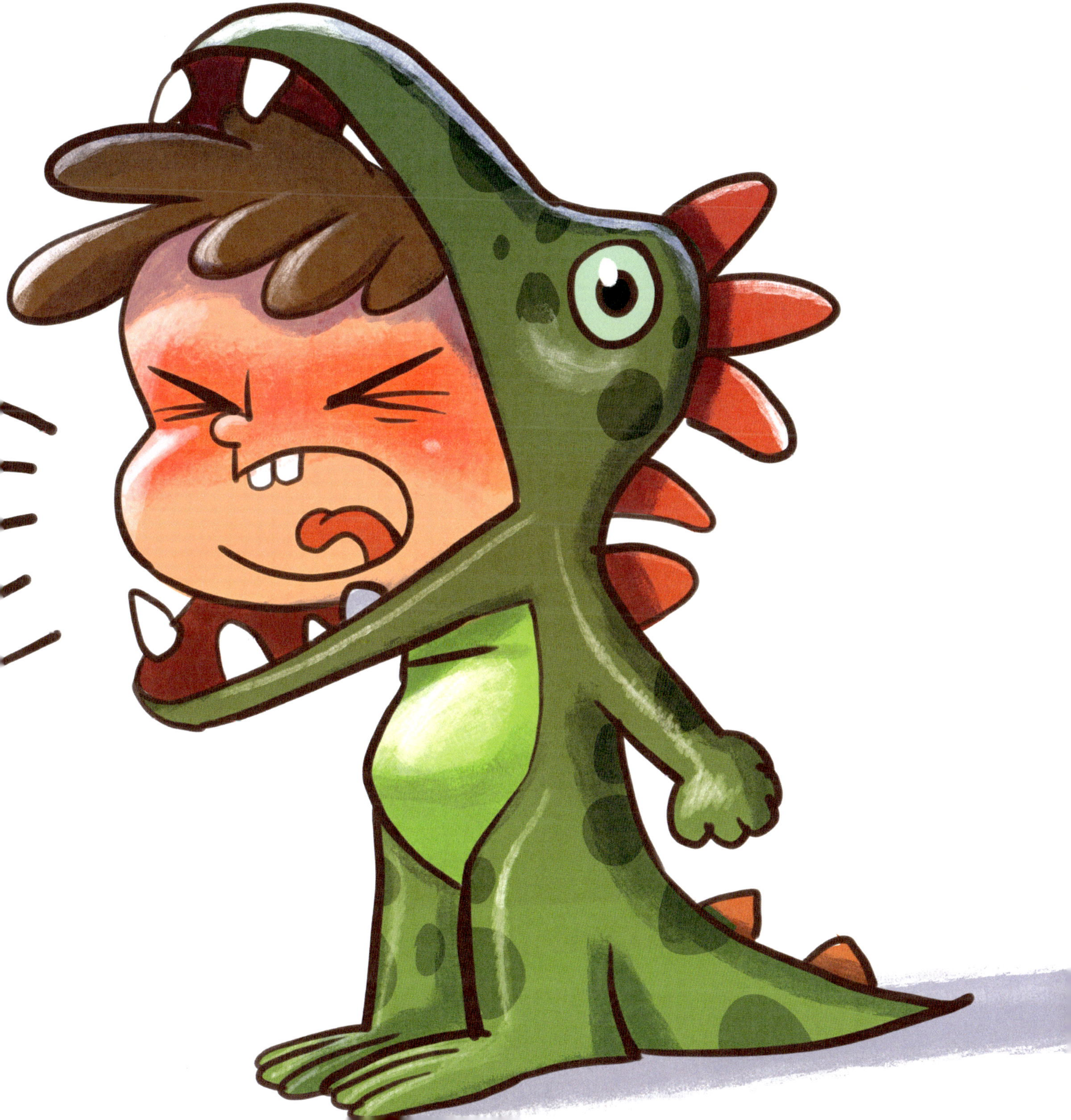

Josh told Mom her idea worked; he no longer felt mad.

But he was tired and wanted to go home; he was now feeling sad.

"You need a hug," Mom said, and she squeezed him tight.

That made Josh feel better and he giggled with delight.

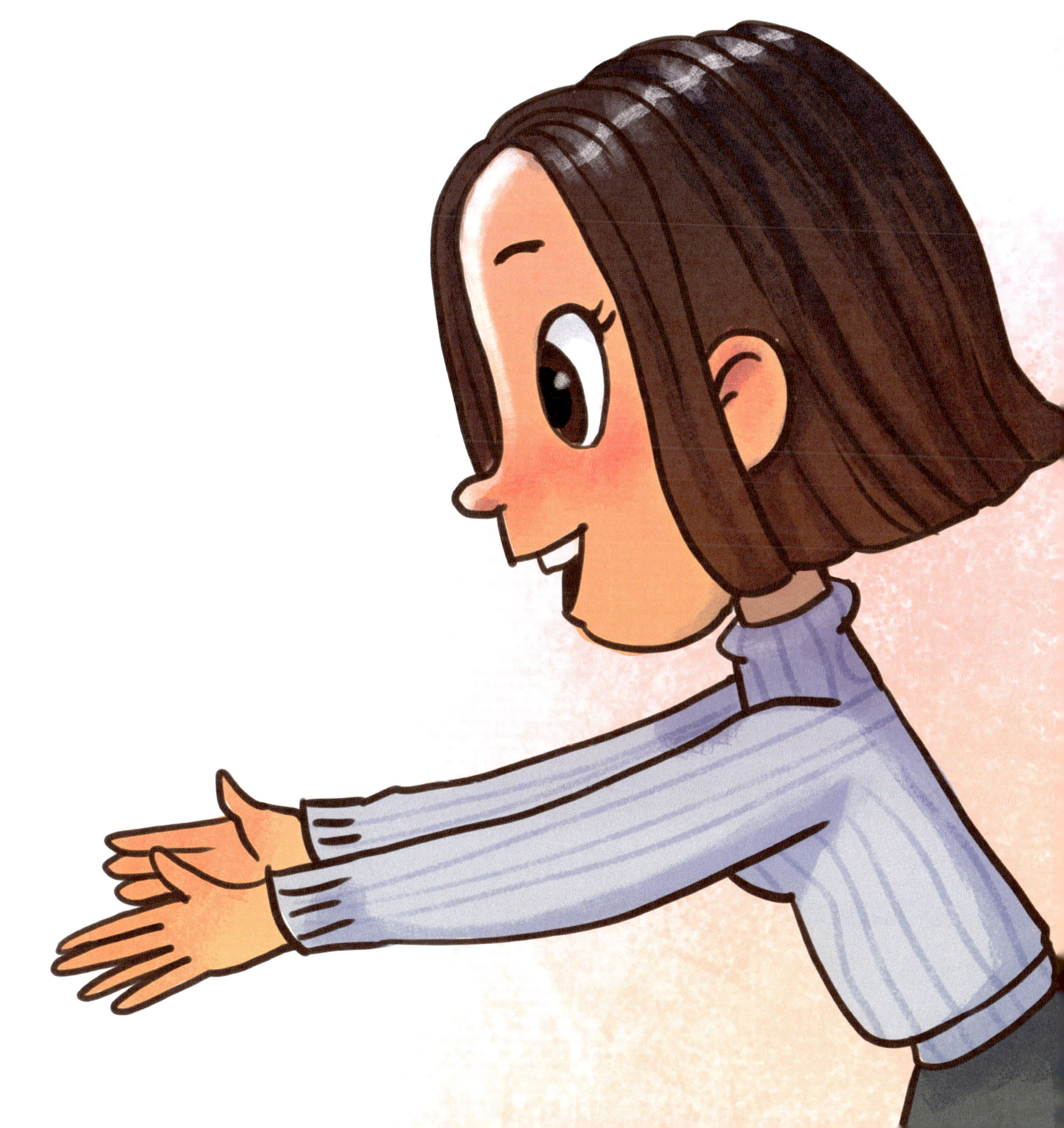

Later, Dad took Josh to the community center to play.

Josh knew just which toy he wanted to play with that day.

At the play center, the big blue truck is his favourite toy.

But this time, it was in the hands of another little boy.

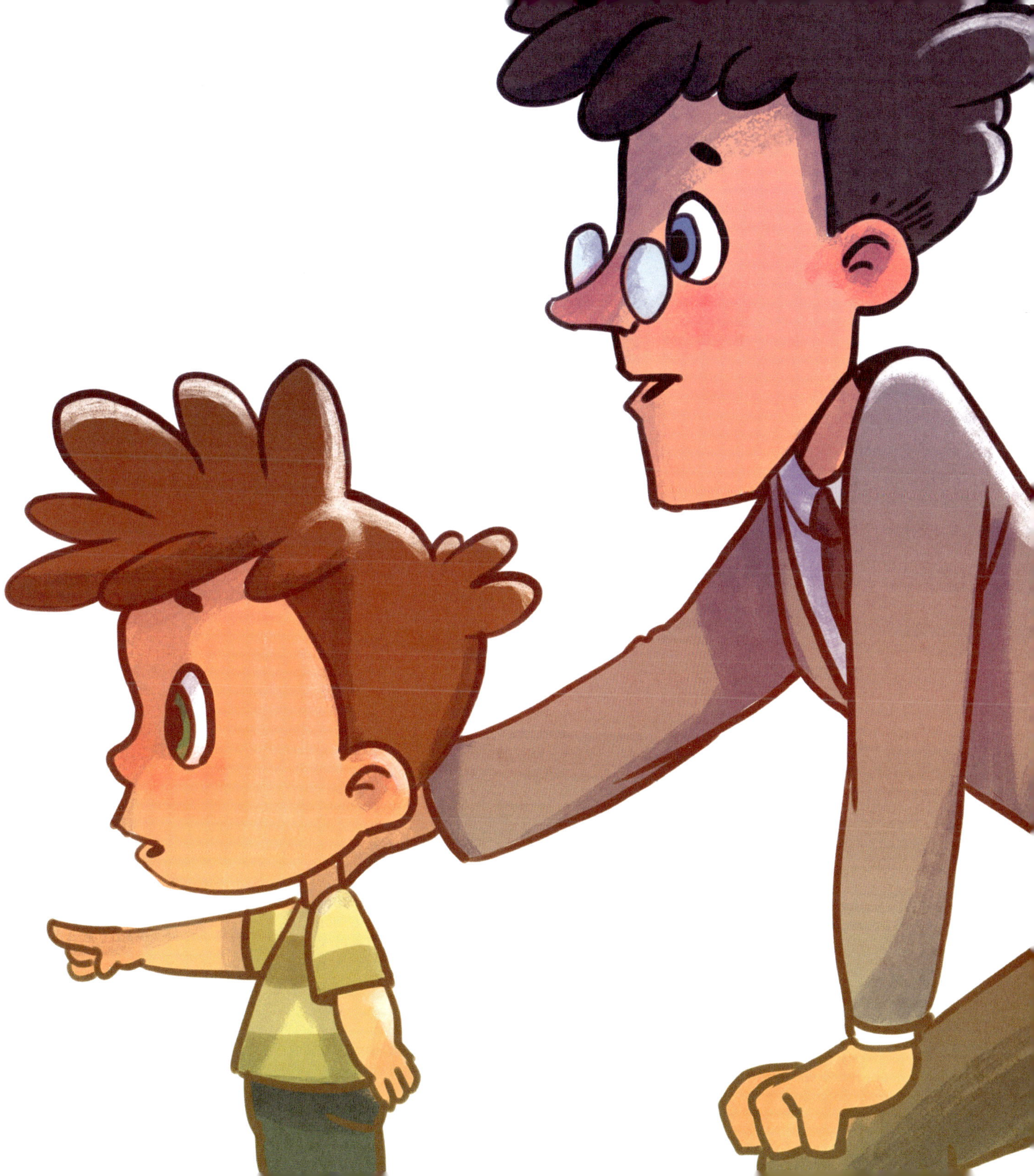

"That's mine!" Josh yelled, as he grabbed onto the truck tight.

"No! I'm playing with it!" The boy yanked back with all his might.

An angry Josh did a dinosaur-stomp back to his dad.

Dad could see right away that Josh was very mad.

"I see a big angry ball inside you, Josh," his dad said.

"That's too much anger to hold on to. It makes you hot and red. Let's throw away some of those balls together as a team."

They threw balls and giggled and Josh let off some anger steam.

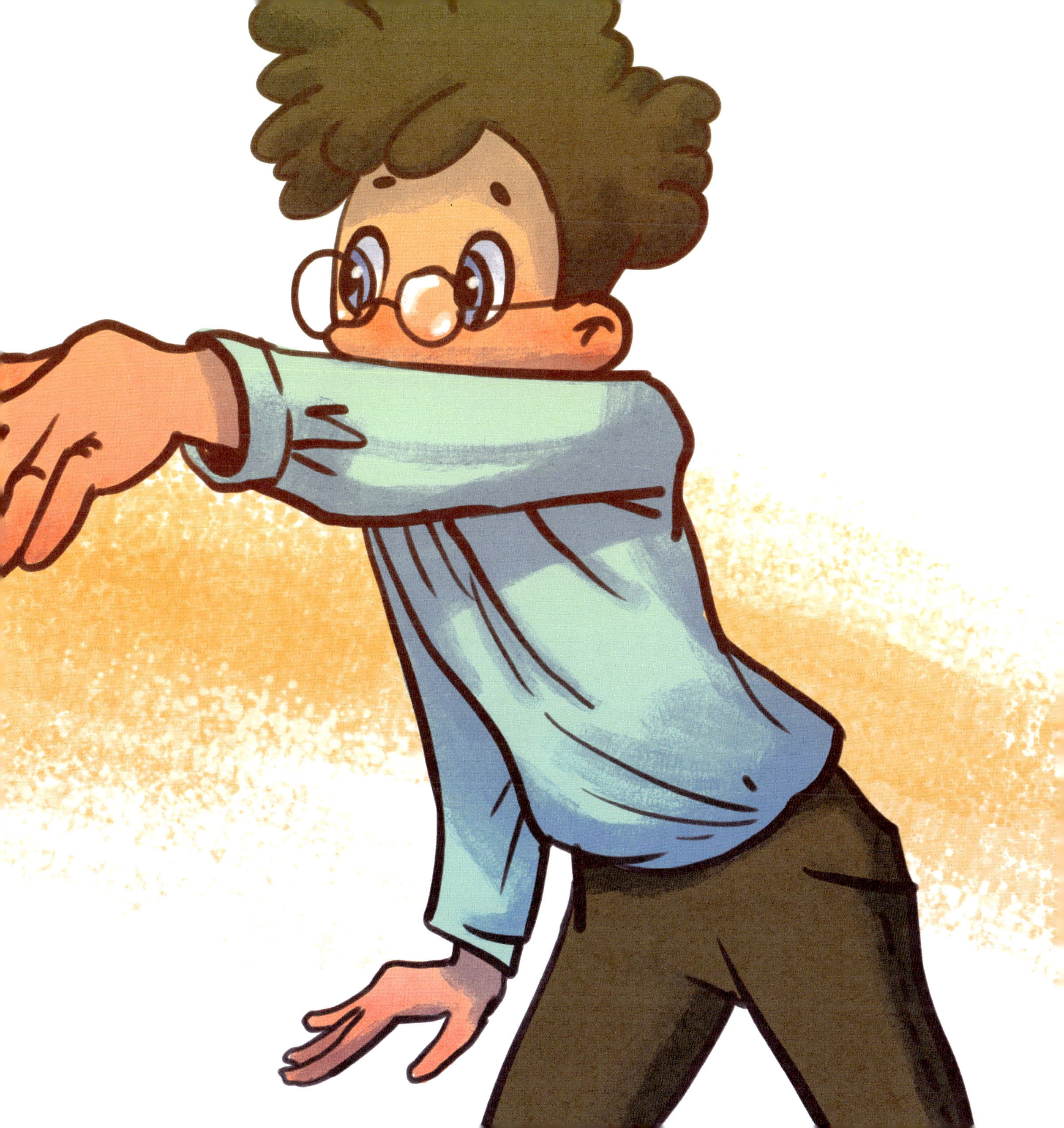

The whole family walked to the park at the end the day.

But when it was time to go home, Josh wanted to stay.

Mom said, "No. We've had lots of fun and now it's getting dark.

Choose one last thing to play on before we leave the park."

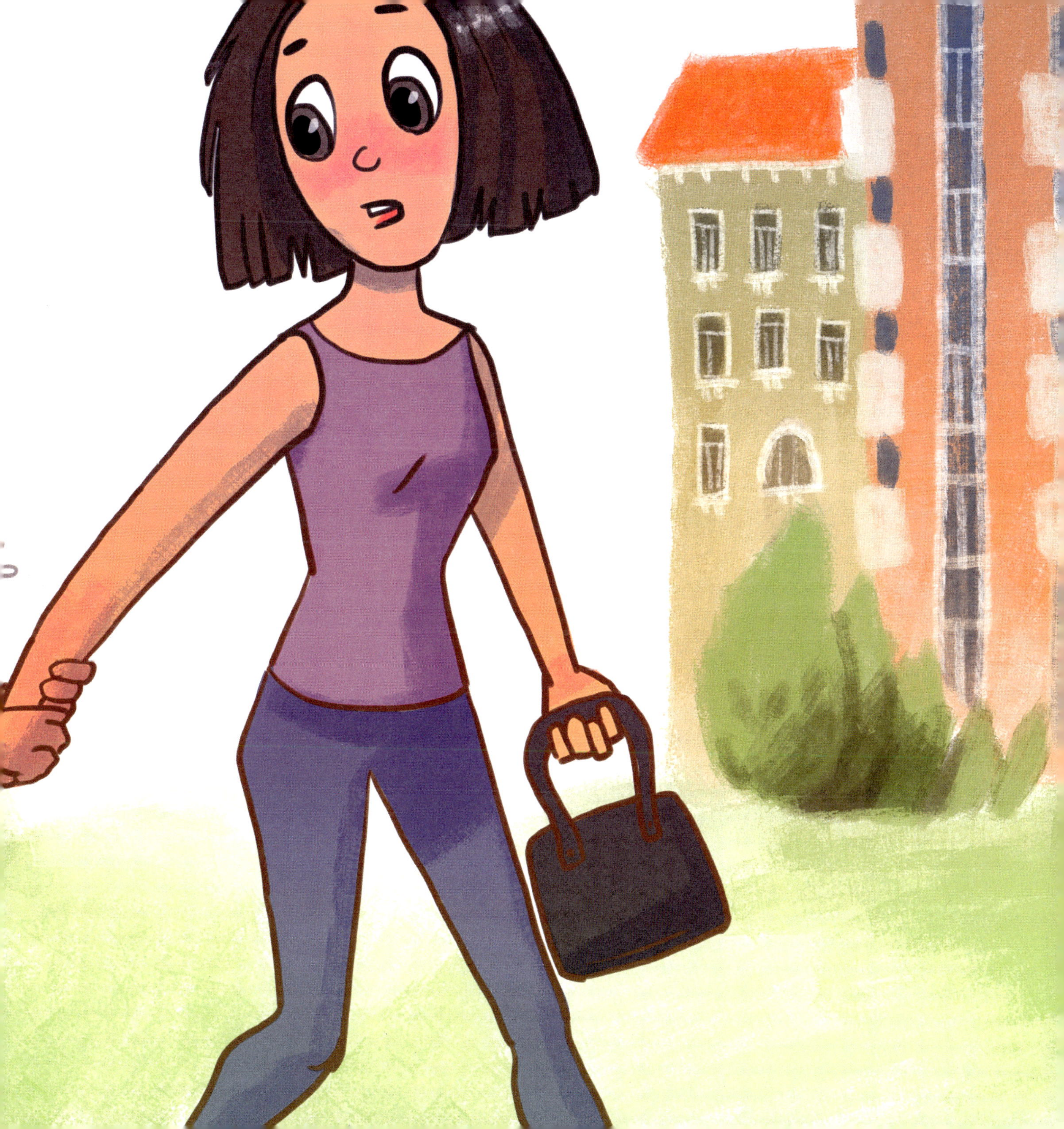

Unsatisfied, Josh was still grumpy as they drove away.
Seeing this, Emma said, "I know a great game we can play.
We'll make our mouths grumpy, and then turn our frowns upside down
With the kind of exaggerated smile you'd see on a clown."

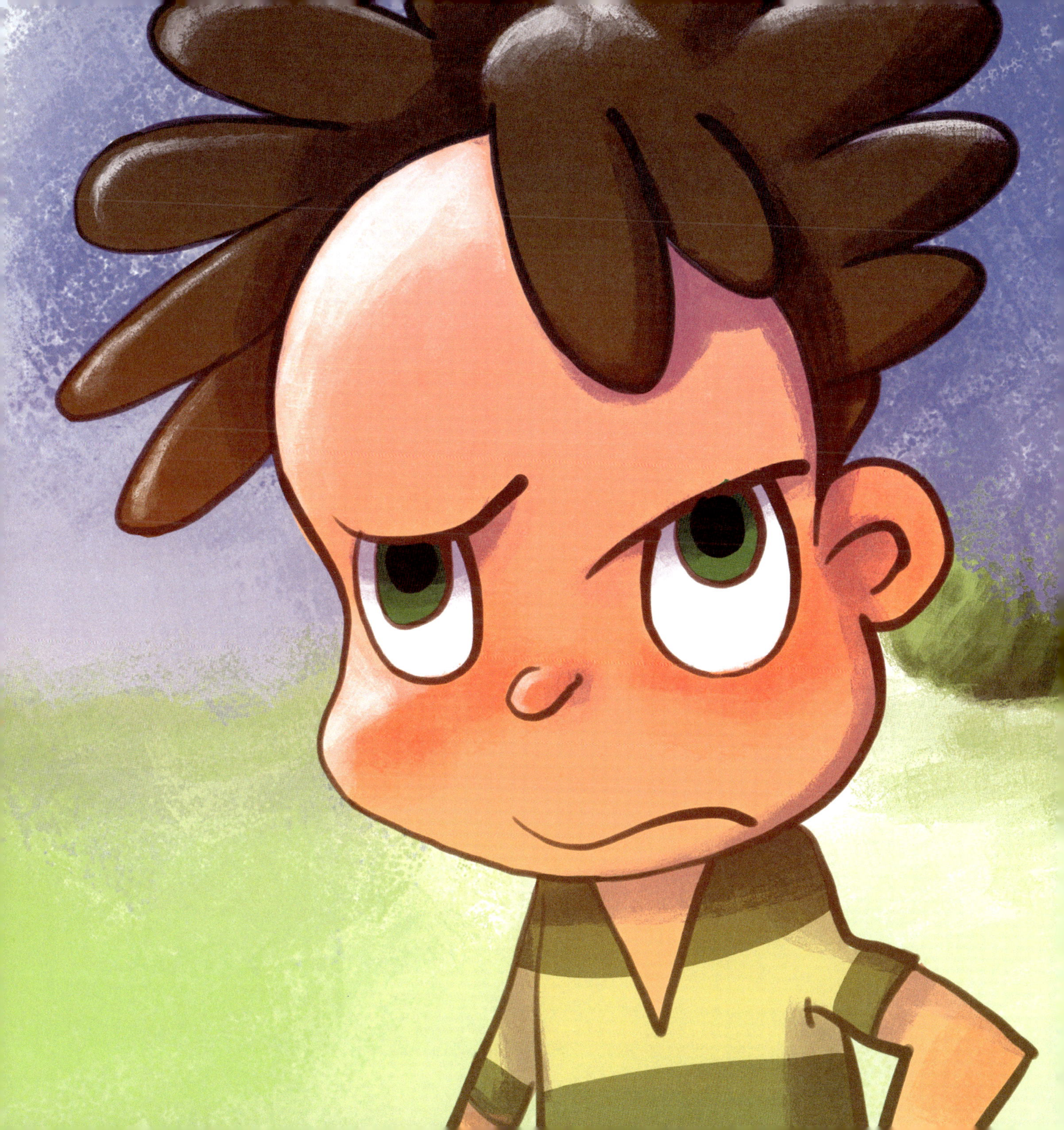

Emma frowned then smiled and their parents did the same.

Josh giggled as he watched everyone play the game.

Smiling, he said, "I've had bad feelings a few times today.

But they never stay long. You all help me make them go away."

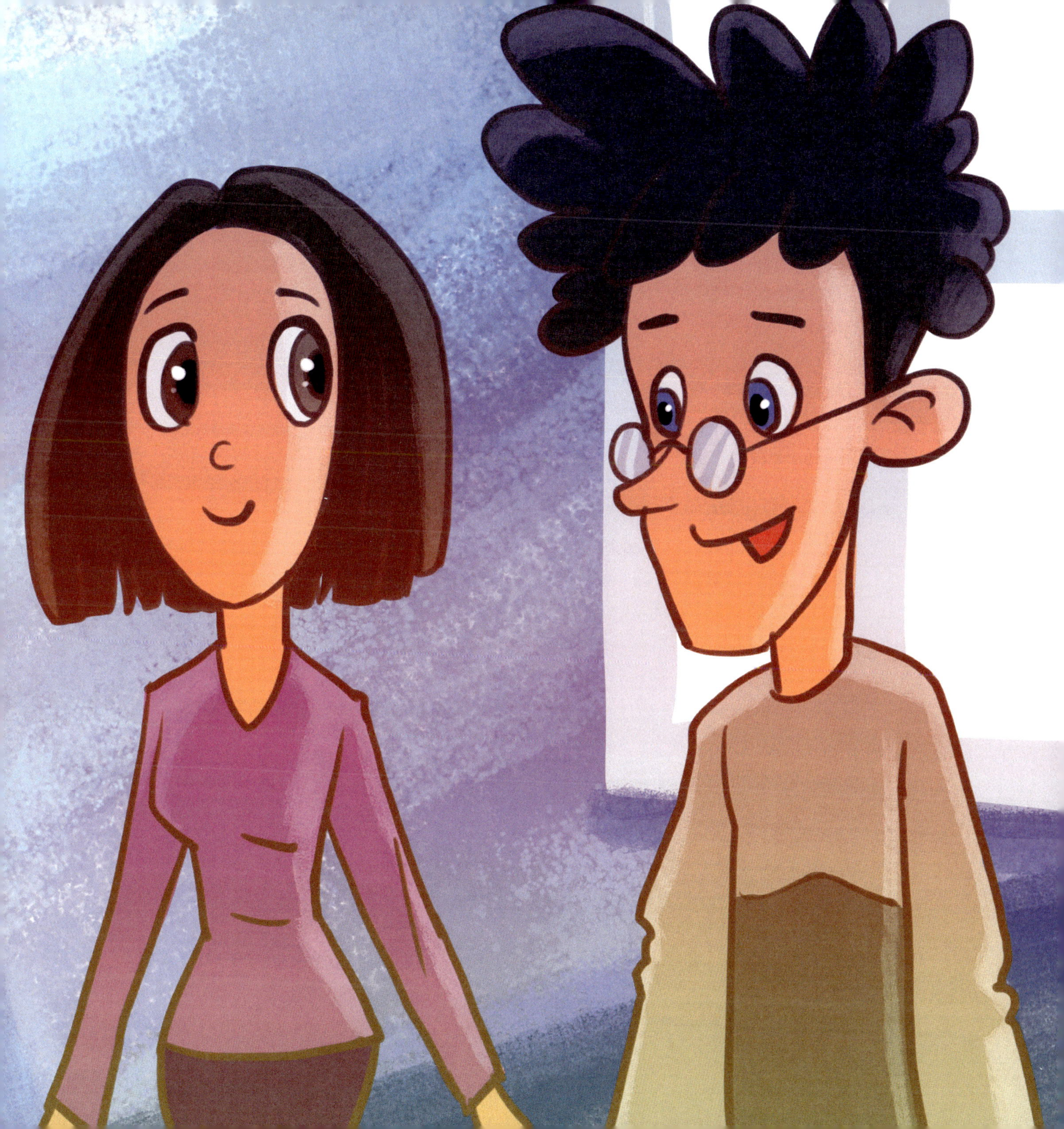

The End

Your opinion could change the word!

I hope you enjoyed this little story. Reviews from awesome customers like you help other parents to feel confident about choosing this book too.

Would you mind taking a minute to leave your feedback?

I will be forever grateful!

Michael

Thank you!

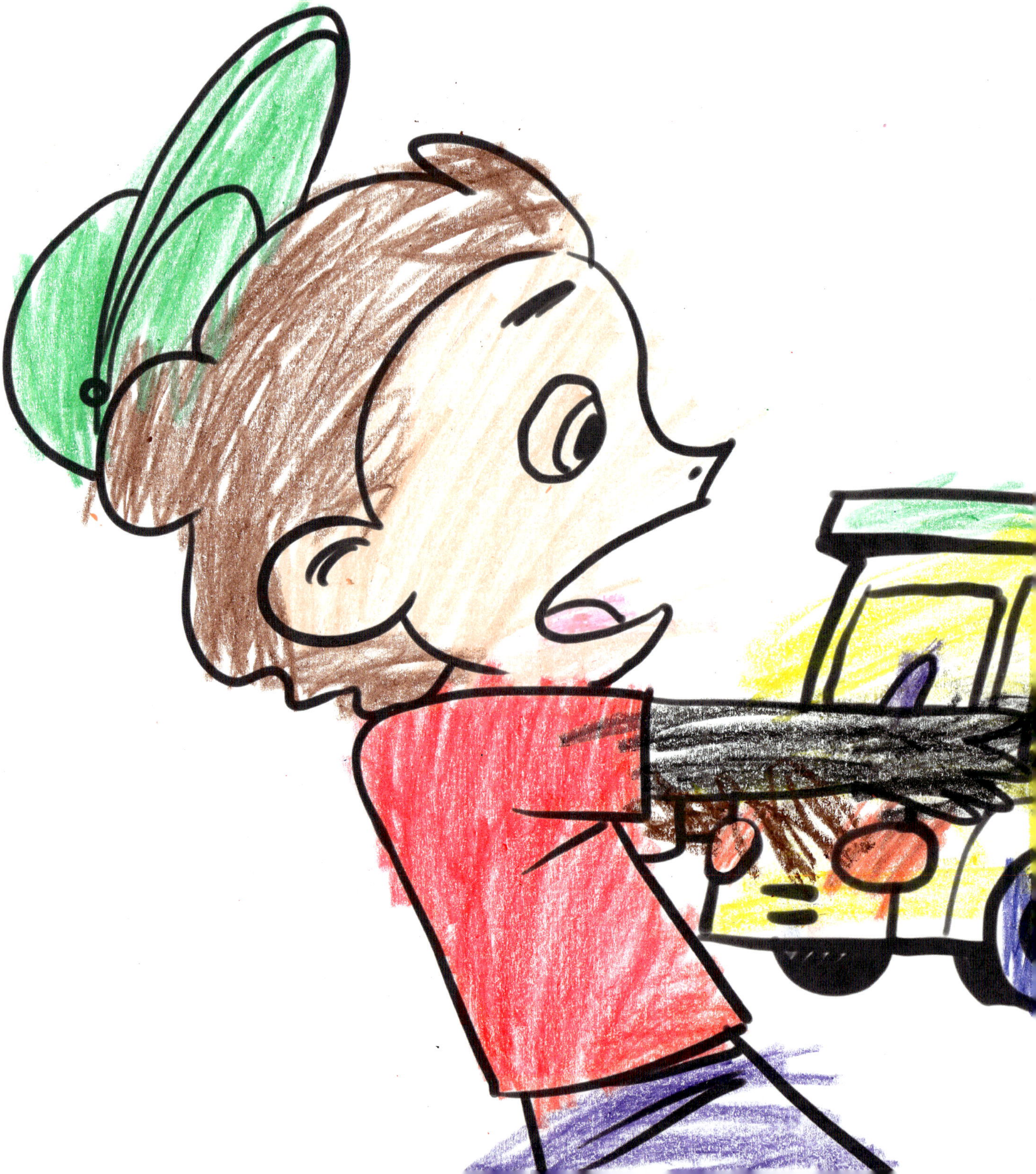

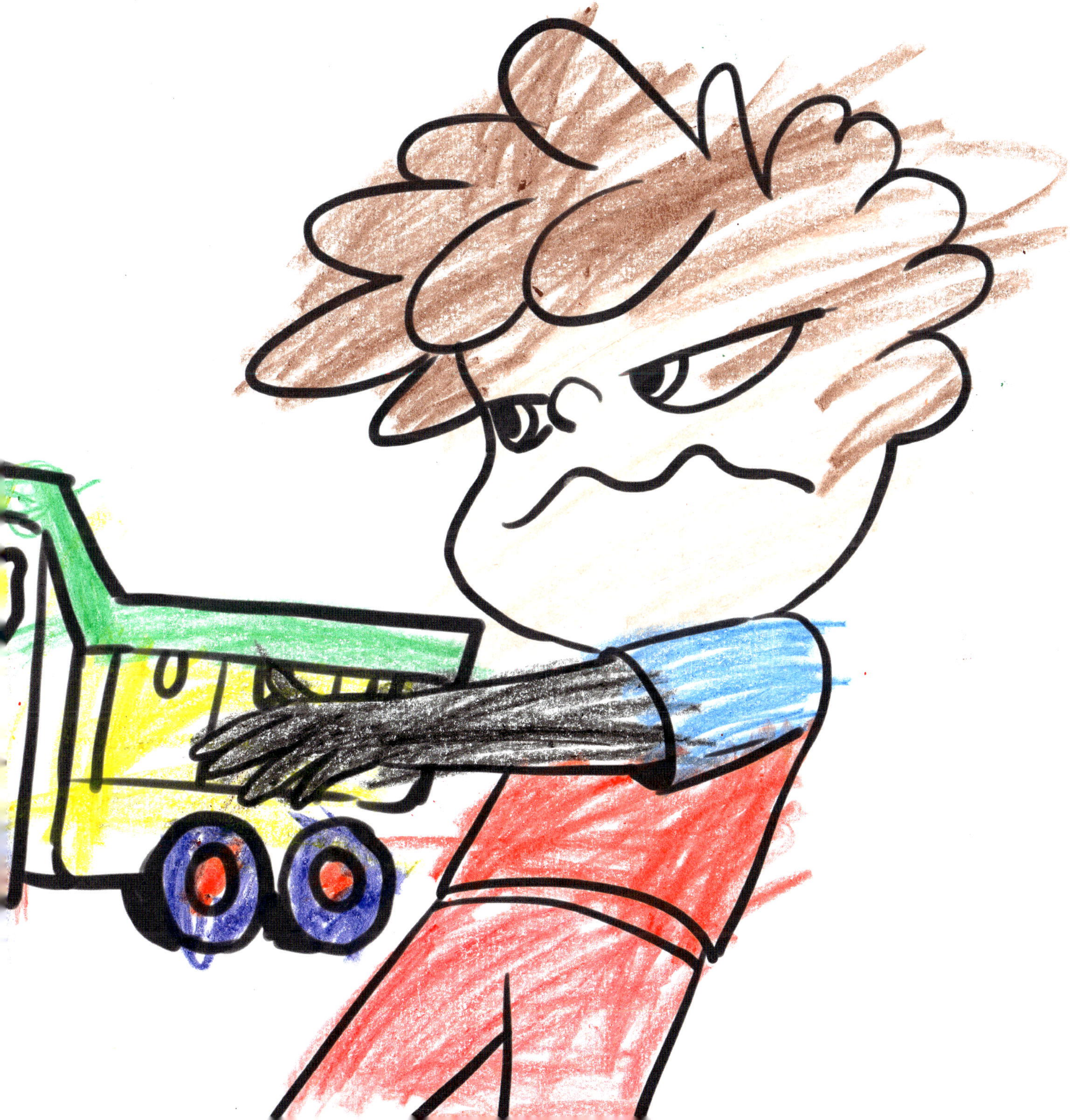

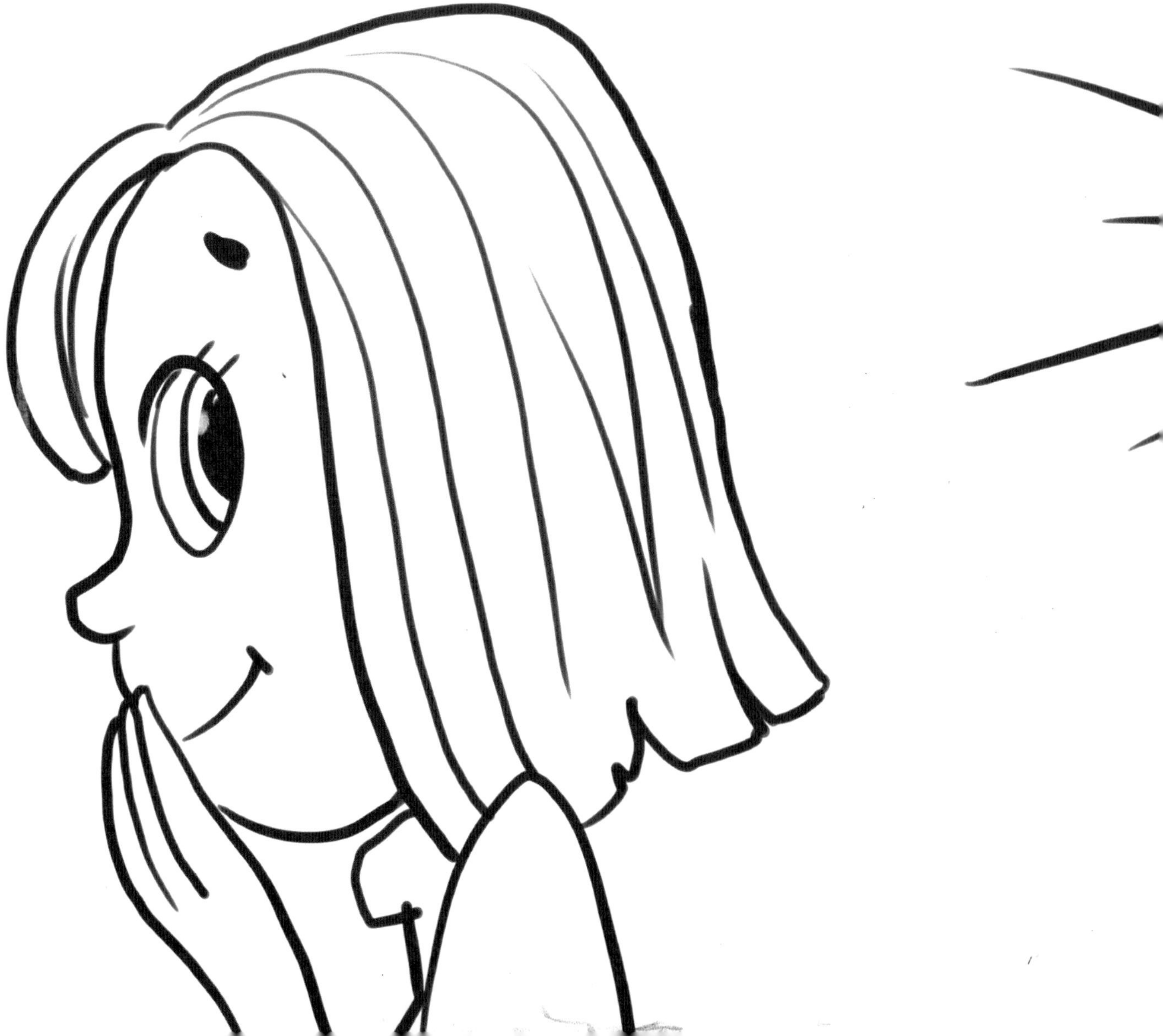

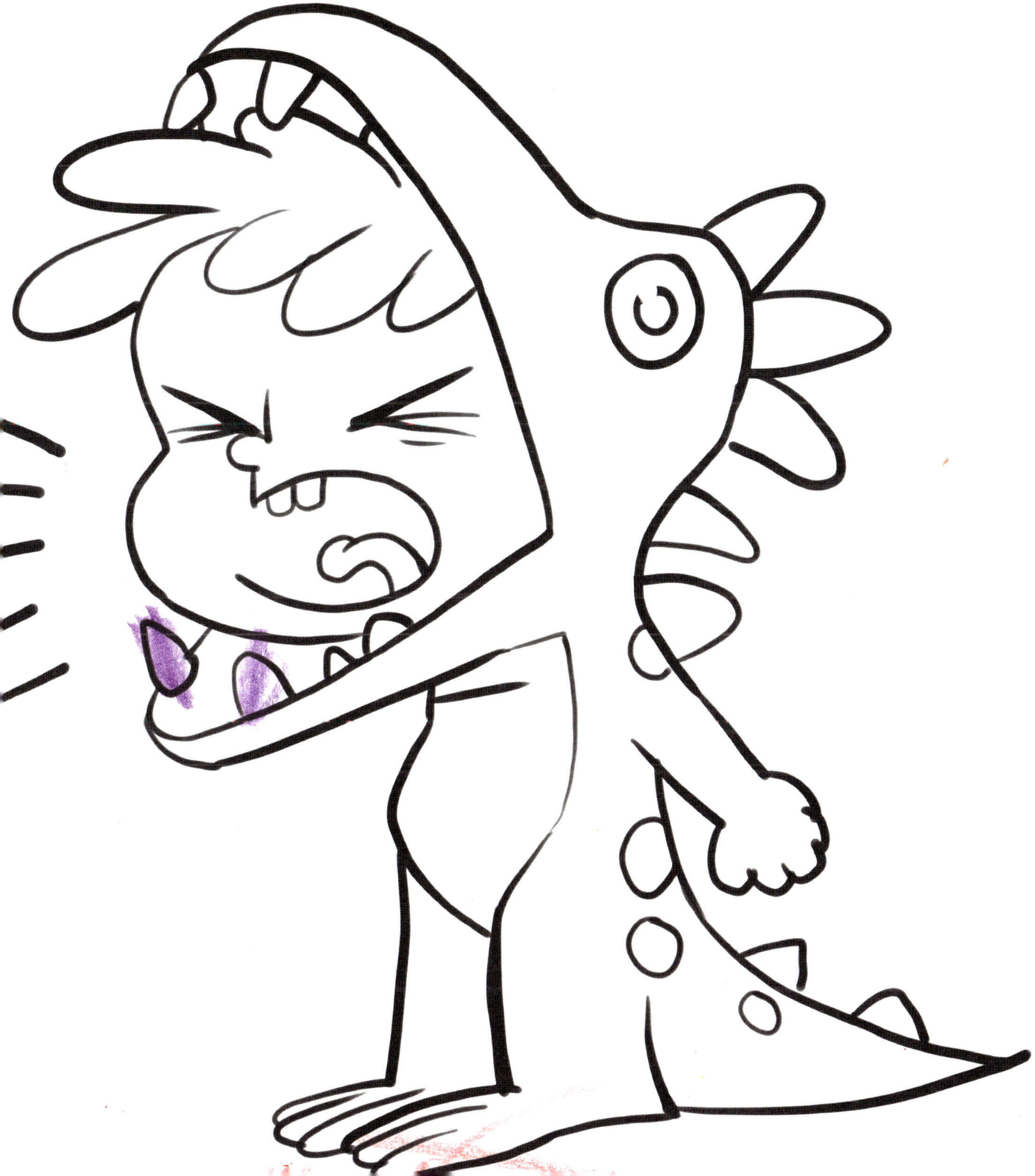

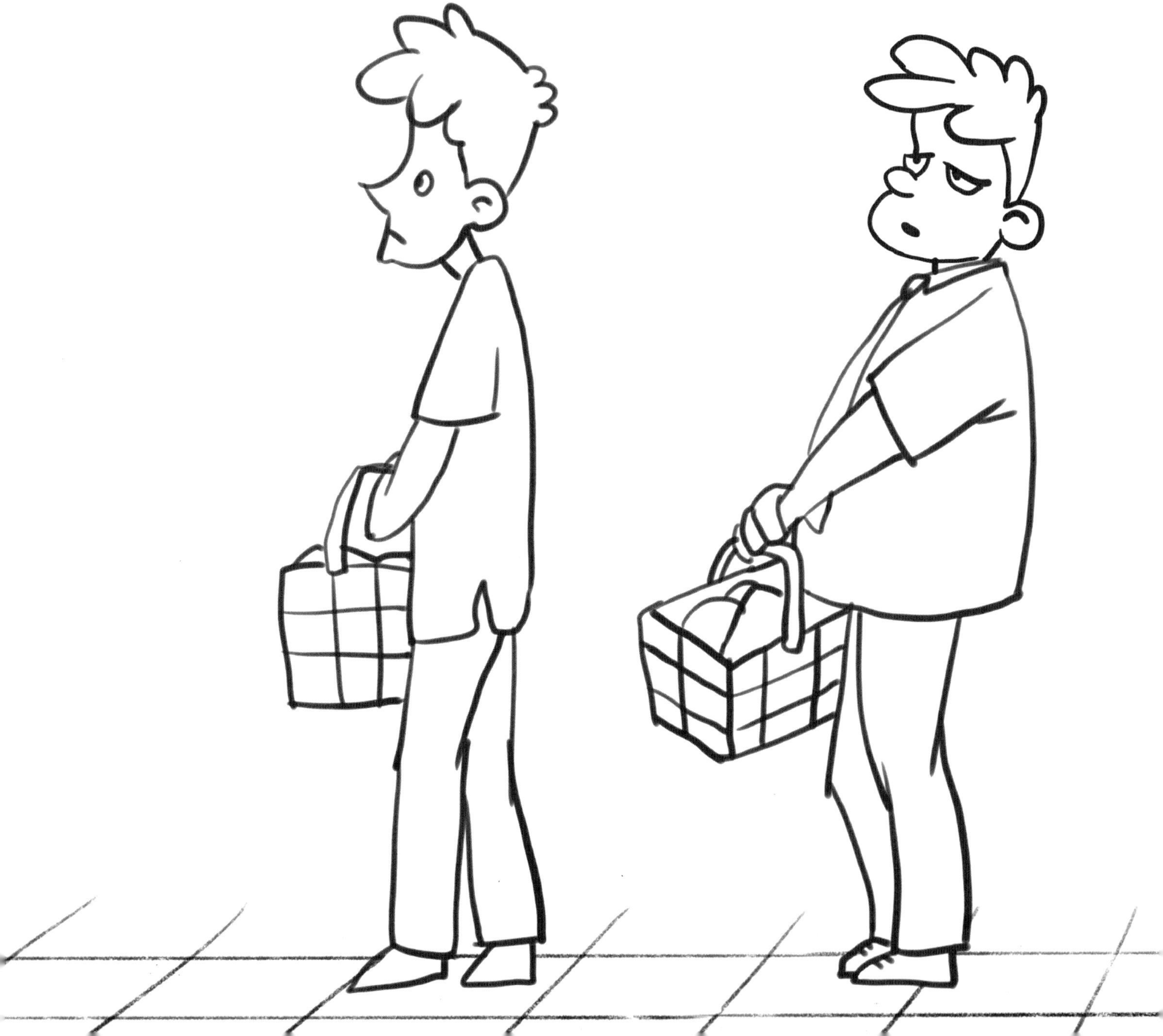

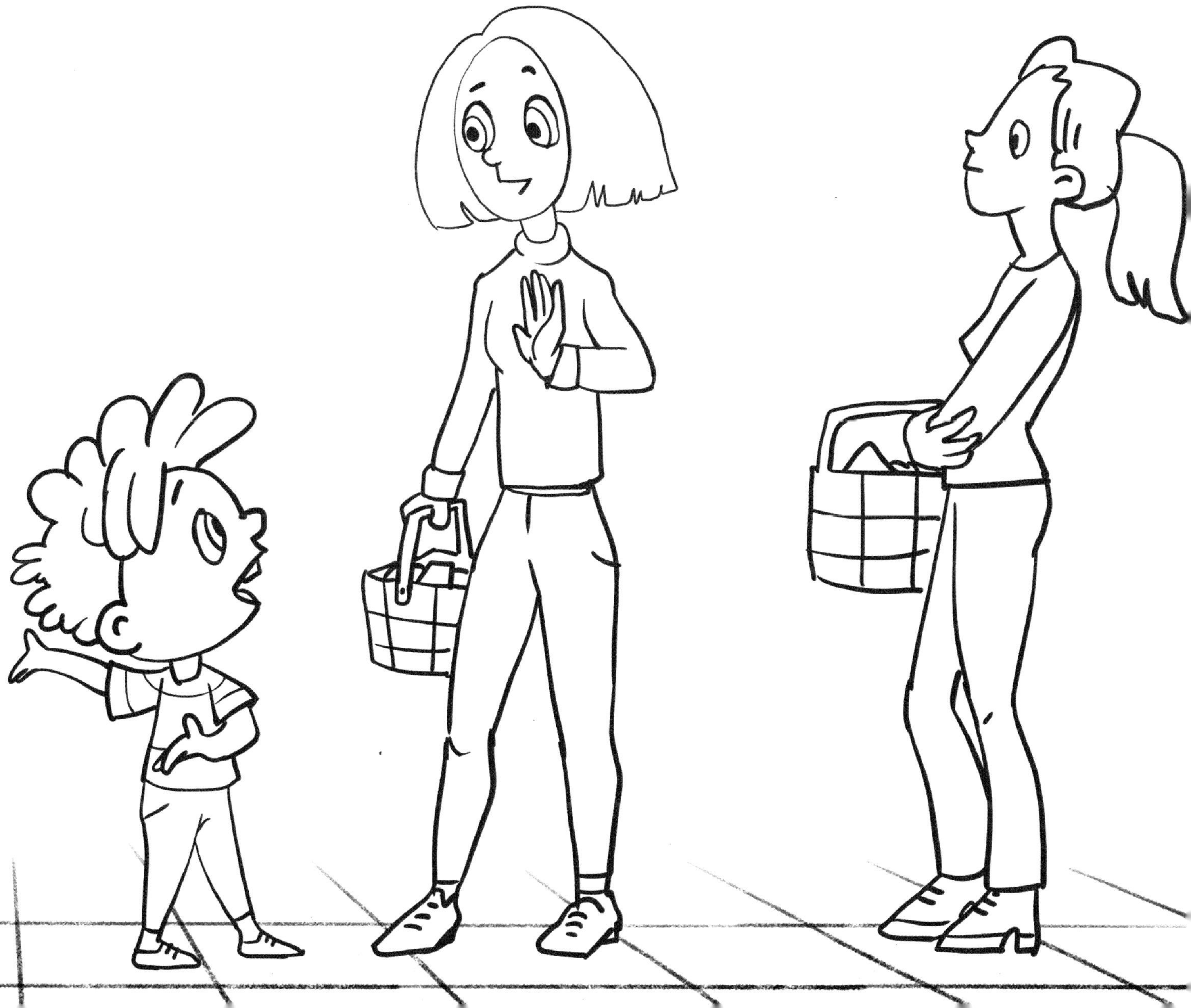

About author

Michael Gordon is the talented author of several highly rated children's books including the popular Sleep Tight, Little Monster, and the Animal Bedtime.

He collaborates with the renowned Kids Book Book that creates picture books for all of ages to enjoy. Michael's goal is to create books that are engaging, funny, and inspirational for children of all ages and their parents.

Contact

For all other questions about books or author, please e-mail michaelgordonclub@gmail.com.

Self-Regulation Skills (7 book series)

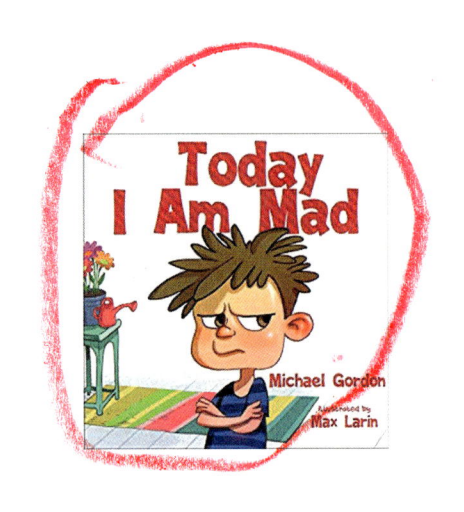

Today I Am Mad

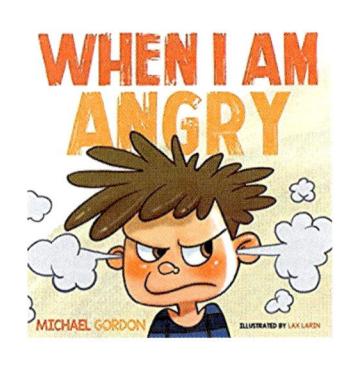

When I am Angry

When I Feel Frustrated

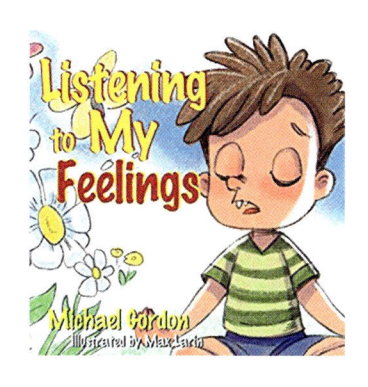

Listening to My Feelings

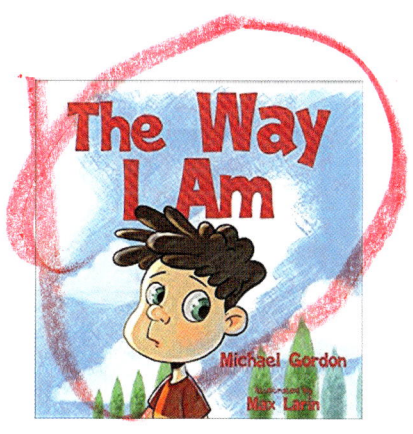

The Way I Am

When I Am Worried

Go https://michaelgordonclub.wixsite.com/books **to get** "The Grumpy Dinosaur" for **FREE!**

Made in the USA
Monee, IL
17 August 2020